Maxwell Mutt

and The DOWNTOWN DOgs

Steve Voake ILLUSTRATED BY Jim Field

WALKER
BOOKS

First published 2016 by Walker Books Ltd
87 Vauxhall Walk, London SE11 5HJ

2 4 6 8 10 9 7 5 3 1

Text © 2016 Steve Voake
Illustrations © 2016 Jim Field

The right of Steve Voake and Jim Field to be identified as
author and illustrator respectively of this work has been asserted by them
in accordance with the Copyright, Designs and Patents Act 1988

This book has been typeset in Goudy Educational

Printed and bound in Great Britain
by Clays Ltd, St Ives plc

British Library Cataloguing in Publication Data:
a catalogue record for this book is available from the British Library

ISBN 978-1-4063-5753-0

www.walker.co.uk

Maxwell Mutt

and The Downtown Dogs

Also by Steve Voake:

Daisy Dawson
Daisy Dawson and the Secret Pool
Daisy Dawson and the Big Freeze
Daisy Dawson at the Seaside
Daisy Dawson on the Farm

Hooey Higgins and the Shark
Hooey Higgins and the Tremendous Trousers
Hooey Higgins and the Big Boat Race
Hooey Higgins Goes for Gold
Hooey Higgins and the Big Day Out
Hooey Higgins and the Awards of Awesomeness
Hooey Higgins and the Storm
Hooey Higgins and the Christmas Crash

CHAPTER ONE

BeginNings

In all his short life, Maxwell Mutt had never known anyone be kind to him. At three weeks old he was sold to a man called Dabsley for a pint of beer and a packet of crisps.

When Dabsley got home he took off his hat and pushed Maxwell into a corner.

"You sit there quiet," he said, flicking a baked bean from his yellow checked scarf. Then he settled down on the sofa to watch a film about cowboys. But, even for a dog, Maxwell's hearing was unusually sensitive and loud noises frightened him.

So when the cowboys started shooting, he cowered
in the corner and howled.

"Hey!" said Dabsley. "I thought I told you to
shut up!"

Then he dragged Maxwell to the cupboard under
the stairs and slammed the door.

The noise frightened Maxwell so much that he
ran to the back of the cupboard and hid.

He shivered alone in the darkness, wondering
what was to become of him.

That night he heard a strange, wonderful sound. It sounded almost like crying but it was more than that; it shimmered and soared and sang in his bones.

He sat at the back of the cupboard and listened, hardly daring to breathe.

But then it was gone and the only noise was Dabsley snoring, fast asleep on the sofa in his big white pants.

The next day, Dabsley came home with a handful of picture cards.

"Right, Mutt!" he said, dragging Maxwell out into the light. "Let's see if your face fits!"

But as he stared at the cards, Dabsley became more and more upset. His eyes narrowed. He shook his head and his cheeks wobbled like strawberry puddings.

"What a waste of money!" he shouted, his face growing redder and redder. "You're not even on the cards! You're not on a single one of them!"

In a rage, he snatched a plate up from the kitchen table and threw it across the room. Maxwell ducked and it shattered on the wall above his head.

Maxwell had no idea what any of this meant.

He crept behind the sofa and stared at the broken plate.

On the fourth day there was a knock at the door and a thin, pale-faced man appeared holding a sack. His hands were trembling and Maxwell saw that he wasn't much more than a boy.

"Ferris!" said Dabsley. "About time. Have you got what I asked for?"

"I think so," said Ferris nervously.

He shook the sack and a small dog fell out. She was wearing a blue collar with a golden tag around her neck.

She yelped in surprise and stared up at Dabsley.

"Take me home," she demanded. "Take me home right now!"

Even if the men had heard her, they wouldn't have understood.

But Maxwell understood perfectly.

Dabsley picked up the small dog and examined her.

"Hey!" she said. "Put me down!"

But Dabsley just stared at the cards spread out on the table and turned to Ferris.

"She ain't on the cards either, you idiot! Now we'll have to get rid of them both!"

"Stop!" barked Maxwell, running out from behind the sofa. "Leave her alone!"

"Quit yelping, you useless hound!" shouted Dabsley. He picked Maxwell up by the scruff of the neck, threw him in the cupboard and slammed the door. Lifting one ear, Maxwell heard the sound of footsteps followed by a door closing.

After a while a small voice whispered, "Hello in there. What's your name?"

Maxwell padded softly to the door.

"I'm Maxwell," he said.

"My name's Paisley," replied the voice. "Sorry you got locked in the dark."

Maxwell heard scratching, followed by small thumps, one after the other.

"What are you doing?" he asked.

"Trying to get you out," said Paisley.

Thump.

"Almost."

Thump.

"Nearly."

Thump.

"Next one should do it."

Maxwell was puzzled. Why would such a small dog think she could break through a thick wooden door? He was still wondering this twenty minutes later when there was a clunk and the door swung open to reveal Paisley hanging from the handle by her teeth.

When she saw Maxwell she let go and dropped to the floor.

"Here he comes," she said. "Back to the light."

Maxwell stared at her. "That's incredible," he said. "How did you do that?"

"Friends never give up," said Paisley. "Didn't anyone ever teach you that?"

CHAPTER TWO

Deep wateR

That night Maxwell listened to Paisley breathing softly in the dark. Already he felt stronger and less afraid. He remembered the strange sound he had heard and for the first time a feeling of hope stirred in his heart.

Now Paisley was here, life would be better.

He rested his head on his paws and closed his eyes.

But as he drifted in and out of dreams he heard the creak of floorboards.

Then Dabsley leapt from the shadows,
grabbed both dogs and threw them in
a sack.

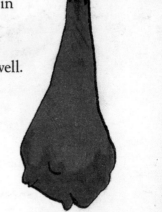

"What's happening?" cried Maxwell.

He listened to the slamming of
doors and suddenly it felt as if
everything good was coming to
an end.

It was raining hard when the van stopped on
the bridge.

"You know what to do," said Dabsley.

"Maybe we should let them go," said Ferris,
whose heart was young and not as dark as
Dabsley's.

But Dabsley just scowled. "Do it," he said.
"And do it properly."

"I want to go home," whispered Paisley.

And although Maxwell didn't know how, he placed his paw over hers and said, "Then you will. I promise."

Ferris heard the whimpering from the back of the van and wished he was at home in bed. But Dabsley glared at him, so he reached over the back of his seat, picked up the sack and opened the passenger door, stepping out into the wind and rain.

He stood on the bridge and gazed down at the fast-flowing river, feeling the sack wriggle beneath his fingers.

"Everyone deserves a chance," he whispered, untying the rope that Dabsley had knotted around the neck of the sack. Dabsley stared at him through the window and he dropped the sack over the edge, listening for the splash as it hit the water below. Then he got back in the van, wiped the rain from his eyes and turned on the radio so he wouldn't have to think about what he had done.

The shock of hitting the cold water was so great that Maxwell gave a startled yelp, his paws scrabbling against the inside of the sack in an effort to free himself. But the river was in full flow and within seconds they were underwater, fighting for their lives. As the current swept them downstream, Maxwell grabbed at Paisley's collar and tore at the neck of the sack with his paws, tumbling out into the black, churning water.

High above him, stars glittered in the midnight sky
and a silver moon shone down upon the chimney
pots of the sleeping city. Maxwell just had time
to breathe cool air before the water swept over
his head and pulled him down into the darkness.
For a few moments, he was so overwhelmed that
he stopped struggling and allowed himself to be
dragged down to the weeds and stones, twisting
and tumbling along the murky river bed. For most
small dogs, this would have been the end of things.

But this was not *any* small dog.

This was Maxwell Mutt.

And although it would be a while before Maxwell knew what the world was about, he had caught a glimpse of the moon and the stars. He had seen the buildings, trees and alleyways and he ached to walk among them and know what it meant to be alive. So Maxwell Mutt reached up with his paws, and broke through the surface, and swam with all his might towards the lights of the city.

 It was only when he reached the riverbank that he saw Paisley's empty collar and realized she was gone.

In the distance he heard the rumble of trains, the shrieking of sirens and, beneath it all, the rush and flow of the river.

Maxwell remembered the strength of the water and wondered how fast and far Paisley had been taken. He looked at the shadowy streets and wondered how many things there were in this strange and endless world. He wondered if, somewhere among them, she might still be alive.

And then, as he remembered his promise, the wind blew a shred of cloud across the moon and he heard a sound like someone crying, somewhere on the other side of the river.

CHAPTER THREE

Cats

Lifting one ear, Maxwell tried to filter out the noise of the city so that he could hear the new sound more clearly. It wasn't easy, but in the gaps between the taxi horns and diesel engines he heard it again. It was a kind of howling, like someone in pain, but there was something beautiful about it too; something familiar. He realized it was the sound he had heard the night before Paisley arrived, and his heart ached for the friend he had lost.

If only he could find out where it came from, maybe he could find her too.

Standing up on his hind legs, Maxwell gazed across the river and watched the headlights flow across the bridge. The sound seemed to come from the far side of the city, where the sky was bathed in an orange glow. Then it was gone and all Maxwell could hear was the roar of traffic and the sigh of the wind, flipping through old newspapers and drawing patterns in the dust.

Although he could no longer hear the sound, he knew he *had* heard it. Picking up Paisley's collar, he slipped through a hole in a fence and padded along a narrow footpath where dandelions hung their heads and slept. He crossed the pavement and turned into a dark alley, still listening for the sound he hoped would somehow lead him back to his friend.

On either side of him were brick walls and gates leading to silent, moonlit gardens. Maxwell sniffed the air and was rewarded with the smell of stale biscuits, chicken bones and the remains of a pepperoni pizza. His stomach rumbled. He hadn't eaten for days. Licking his lips, he followed the scent to a dustbin at the end of the alley.

But as he placed a paw against it, the lid shot off and a ginger cat stared at him from the shadows.

"Thievin' me bits n' pieces, is it?" hissed the cat. "Stealin' Ginger's scoggins?"

Maxwell stepped back and dropped Paisley's collar in the dirt.

"I'm not stealing anything," he said. "I've come to look for my friend."

"Got a face like a pizza, have he?" said Ginger. "Made out of biskies and chicky bones and answers to the name of Ginger's Scoggins?"

"*Her* name's Paisley," said Maxwell nervously. "And if you haven't seen her then I'll be on my way."

"I don't think so," said Ginger. He flipped his paw over and five razor-sharp claws sprang out, glinting in the moonlight. "Them's me rippers," he said. "And here come some more."

"I'm not looking for trouble," said Maxwell, taking a few steps back.

"Too late," said Ginger. "You found it."

Maxwell heard the scrape of bin lids and saw half a dozen cats slink down the alley, their green eyes gleaming in the darkness. As they hissed and spat their way towards him, Maxwell thought he heard the whisper of different voices, somewhere beyond the alley. But as he lifted his ears to listen, a scraggy cat sprang from the shadows and dug its claws into his back.

"Got 'im!" it screeched, scratching and biting until Maxwell lost his footing and fell to the floor.

"Out of me way!" hissed Ginger. "It's time for some lesson learnin'!"

But as the others drew back, there was a growl from the end of the alley and a voice shouted,

"STEP AWAY FROM THE DOG! STEP AWAY FROM THE SMALL DOG AND NO ONE GETS HURT!"

CHAPTER FOUR

Dogs

The cats froze, their mouths hanging open.

"OK, LiSTEN UP!" called the voice. "We have you surrounded! One false move and you'll spend the rest of the night picking your teeth out of the wall.

Am I making myself clear?"

"Moww," mumbled a few of the cats, staring down at their paws.

"I can't hear you," said the voice. "I said: **AM i MAKiNG MYSELF CLEAR?**"

"Moww!" shouted the cats, nodding their heads furiously. "Moww, moww, moww!"

"I should think so too," said the voice. "OK son, make your way up the alley, nice and slow."

Maxwell squinted into the darkness and saw a large grey-brown Alsatian standing in the shadows. Crouching beside it was a cream-coloured bulldog wearing a red collar with pointy studs.

As Maxwell approached, it stood on its hind legs and gave him a cheery wave.

"Hiyaa! How's it going?"

Maxwell shook himself and sat next to a dustbin overflowing with rubbish. "Thank you," he said. "I think you just saved my life."

"No need to thank me, son," said the Alsatian, holding up his paw. "Just doing my job."

The bulldog looked at him. "You don't *have* a job."

"Yes I do." The Alsatian stood to attention and put a paw against his head. "Police Dog Restreppo number four–six–five, serving the community since the summer of 2012."

The bulldog rolled his eyes and turned to Maxwell. "He *used* to be a police dog but they retired him, although he won't have it. Which is why we're out chasing cat-faced crims when we should be back in Denby Street sleeping in our baskets."

"Denby Street?" asked Maxwell. "Where's that?"

"It's where we live," said the bulldog. "A much classier part of town. I'm actually on the lookout for some new fabric to go with all the lovely things in my fabulous home. Something in a lemony yellow, perhaps. You haven't seen any, have you?"

Maxwell shook his head.

"Oh well, not to worry." The bulldog leaned against the wall, puffed out his cheeks and popped them with his paws.

"Oh, *don't* do that," said Restreppo.

"Why not?"

"Because it's *weird*," said the Alsatian.

"*You're* weird." The bulldog dropped to all fours and looked at Maxwell. "Don't worry about him. He has anger issues."

"I do NOT have anger issues."

"See? Right there," said the bulldog.

In the silence that followed, Maxwell tried to listen for the sound again. But all he could hear was cats whispering and a truck trundling along five streets away.

The bulldog coughed and held out his paw. "The name's Bernard, but my friends call me Mr B."

"I'm Maxwell," said Maxwell, shaking his paw. "I'm trying to find my friend Paisley."

Mr B nodded sympathetically. "Stayed out late, did she? Dancing till dawn?"

Maxwell shook his head. "She was swept away by the river."

"Probably drowned," called one of the cats from down the alley.

"Hey!" growled Restreppo. "Who asked your opinion?"

"Just saying."

"Well don't."

"Umm, can we go now?" called one of the cats. "It's just that some of us have other appointments."

"*Un*-believable," said Mr B. "Cats are so annoying." He wandered over to a pile of old drinks cans and started sorting them into neat piles. "The world is so untidy. All it takes is a little bit of care and attention to keep things in their proper place."

"Paisley isn't in her proper place," said Maxwell. "That's why I need to find her. I heard a strange sound, you see."

"Sorry," said a cat. "Must be the pizza."

"I've had enough of this," said Restreppo.

He cleared his throat. "All right, this is a police announcement. Owing to the fact that they are being annoying in a built-up area, all cats are ordered to leave immediately. Any cat failing to comply in the next three seconds will find

themselves upside down in the nearest dustbin.

Any questions? Right, go."

"I have a qu—"

"ONE..."

"But I wasn't..."

"TWO..."

"Can't we just..."

"THREE!"

The cats stared open-mouthed as Restreppo

bounded down the alley towards them.

But as he got nearer they leapt in the air and screeched over the wall like a bunch of fireworks.

Maxwell watched them disappear and realized that the world was even stranger than he'd imagined.

"A police dog needs clues," said Restreppo when he got back. "Tell me more about this sound."

"It's hard to describe," said Maxwell, "but it reminds me of when I first met Paisley. I think it's coming from somewhere on the other side of the river."

"Well that's an end to it then," said Mr B. "There's a woman over there they call The Collector. They say she chops dogs' heads off and sticks them on the wall."

Maxwell shuddered. "Why would anyone do such a thing?"

"Humans get up to all sorts," said Restreppo.

33

"That's why the world needs police dogs. And my good friend Officer Marshall, of course."

"It's not just humans," said Mr B. "Last week Dachshund Dan went for a walk over there and the East Street Dogs threw him in the duck pond. Now he'll only go to sleep with the light on. He spends most of his time either hiding behind the sofa or drinking out of the toilet bowl."

"We've all done that," said Restreppo. "How's he reach, anyway?"

"Dunno, probably stands on a box. The point is, it's *dangerous* over there."

"But I have to go," said Maxwell. "I have to find Paisley."

"That's the spirit, kid," said a rough, gravelly voice. "Let's all go over and have ourselves a fight."

 Maxwell turned to see a white poodle wearing woollen booties.

The fur on his head was gathered into a top-knot and the rest of his coat had been blow-dried, giving the impression that he had been out in a high wind.

"Ah, Madison," said Mr B. "Why would we want a fight?".

"Why wouldn't we?" replied the poodle.

Mr B looked at Madison's paws. "Still wearing your little blue booties, I see. Very fetching."

"At least I'm not wearing a second-hand collar," said Madison.

Mr B gasped and staggered back against the wall. "This is *not* a second-hand collar! My owners got it from Collar Me Beautiful!"

35

"That's another thing," said Madison. "How come we've never *met* your owners? How come we've never been invited over?"

"Maybe they're just very *particular*," said Mr B. "Maybe they don't like dogs with stupid haircuts."

"Or second-hand collars," said Madison. He pretended to cough and muttered *"Found it in a dustbin."*

"i DiD NOT FiND iT iN A DUSTBiN!" howled Mr B. **"TELL HiM, RESTREPPO!"**

"Maybe we should all just calm down a bit," said Restreppo.

"Or maybe we should just do *this*," said Madison, kicking over Mr B's pile of cans.

As the dogs continued to argue, Maxwell slipped quietly away and kept walking until he reached the river.

For a long time he stared across the water at the houses and factories and schools and churches, watching their lights twinkle in the darkness. Then, somewhere between the earth and sky, he heard the sound again.

"I'll find you, Paisley," he whispered. "I promise I'll find you."

CHAPTER FIVE

Rats

"Don't jump!" squeaked a voice and Maxwell turned to see two small rats standing behind him. The first one stepped forward, balancing itself with its tail.

"Royston jumped in the river last week and nearly drowned."

"It's true," admitted Royston. "I thought I saw some cheese, but it was a reflection of the moon."

"Easy mistake to make," said the first rat, whose name was Ridley. "You start out looking for one thing and end up finding another."

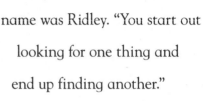

He stared at Maxwell in the half-light. "You're a big rat, if you don't mind me saying so."

"I'm not a rat, I'm a dog," replied Maxwell. "My name's Maxwell and I'm looking for my friend."

"We're all looking for something," said Ridley. "Tell him, Royston."

Royston made a face. "Do I have to?"

"Come on, we've talked about this."

Royston sighed and pointed to the sky. "There are no limits to our dreams," he said. "If we can dream it, we can do it. And if we can do it, then one day we will find our Camembert."

"Camembert is the cheese in our darkness," explained Ridley. "We had some once, but we lost it."

"I lost my friend in the river," said Maxwell sadly. "I don't know where she is."

"Don't be too down-hearted," said Ridley. "What's lost can be found. And in between the looking, there's always fun to be had."

Royston thought for a moment, then clapped his paws together. "I know! Let's teach him the sounds game!"

Maxwell looked anxiously across the river. "I haven't really got the time," he said.

"There's always time for games," replied Ridley. "Tell him, Royston."

"All you have to do is point to something," explained Royston. "Then the other person has to find a word that sounds like the thing you're pointing at. Just watch and we'll show you how to play."

He pointed upwards. "Sounds like..."

"Sky?" said Ridley.

"Yes!" said Royston. "You see, Maxwell? I pointed to the sky and now

Ridley has to guess a word that sounds like it."

"Fly?"

Royston shook his head.

"My?"

"That's it!" Royston pointed at

Ridley to show he was right.

"OK, Maxwell, your turn," said Royston, curving

his tail between his paws. "Sounds like..."

"Tail," said Maxwell.

"Nope." Royston curved his tail a bit more.

"Bend?"

"Yes! Now you're getting it!" said Royston.

"Sounds like 'bend'."

"Friend," said Maxwell. "My ... *friend*..."

"OK," said Royston. "Last bit."

He cupped his ear. "Sounds

like ... 'Fridley'!"

"Is it Ridley?" asked Maxwell.

41

"Yes it is!" cried Royston. "*My friend Ridley!*"

Ridley looked at Maxwell. "I think I need to teach Royston the rules again," he said.

At that moment there was a high-pitched cheer and Maxwell turned to see a group of rats squeaking and laughing and clapping their paws, all gathered around a large rectangle scratched in the dust.

In the middle of the rectangle were twelve rats, some stretching, some running on the spot and others playing keepy-uppy with a pickled onion. At either end were two lolly sticks planted into the ground.

"Everybody ready?" shouted the referee, banging a teaspoon on the floor.

"YEE-ESS!" squealed the crowd.

The referee dropped the pickled onion and a stocky rat back-heeled it to the centre-forward, who tapped it past a midfielder and raced down the wing towards the defence.

"What are they doing?" whispered Maxwell.

"Playing football," said Ridley. "You have to kick the ball between the posts and score a goal." Seeing the puzzled look on Maxwell's face, he added, "It's another way of having fun when you're not looking for things."

A skinny-looking rat shouted, "On me 'ead, son! On me 'ead!" The centre-forward flicked a long, curving cross that sailed across the goalmouth. Then everything seemed to happen in slow motion.

The skinny rat leapt into the air.

The goalkeeper shouted, **"NOOOOOO!"**

The skinny rat headed the pickled onion and it flew past the goalkeeper and right between the posts.

"GOAL!" roared the crowd.

They danced and whistled and waved their paws, singing:

> "Our team's awesome, our team's great
> Our team's making us cel-e-brate
> Pass us the ball and you can bet
> We're gonna bang that ball in the back of your net!"

Maxwell's stomach rumbled loudly and all the rats turned to look at him.

"Someone's hungry," said Ridley. "Let's see if we can find you some cheese."

He pulled a brown paper bag from a nearby bin and sniffed.

"Ooh, smells like pasty."

"Jackpot!" said Royston. "Go on, Maxwell. Give it a try."

Maxwell pushed his nose into the bag and was met by a wonderful smell that greeted him warmly and told him all was well with the world. He bit into the pasty and a rich, meaty gravy squirted into his mouth. A flurry of flavours tumbled over his tongue and  Maxwell whined and whimpered and wagged his tail, wishing it would go on for ever.

"It's delicious!" he exclaimed through a mouthful of gravy.

"Glad you like it," said Ridley. "We come here a lot, don't we, Royston?"

Royston nodded. "It's our favourite restaurant."

Remembering his manners, Maxwell pushed the bag back towards them.

"Would *you* like some?"

"I'm fine," replied Ridley. "Royston?"

Royston shook his head. "I'm saving myself for the cheese and biscuits."

Maxwell was about to eat some more when he stopped and lifted his ears.

"Ooh, are we playing the sounds game again?" asked Royston. "Sounds like..."

"Cat," said Maxwell.

Royston frowned. "Hat?"

"No, it actually is a cat," said Maxwell.

"Actually–*is*–a–cat," repeated Royston. "Hmm, tricky one."

"I think what Maxwell means," said Ridley, "is that an actual cat is actually coming."

"Oh," said Royston.

47

With a squeak, he ran off to warn the others.

"Cats and rats don't really mix," explained Ridley. He turned to follow Royston, then stopped and looked back.

"Good luck, Maxwell Mutt," he said. "I hope you find what you're looking for."

CHAPTER SIX

Restreppo is uNhappy

As the rats scampered off, Maxwell heard a patter of paws and then a familiar ginger cat leapt out of the shadows.

"Is you again," said the cat.

"It *is* me," agreed Maxwell. "Nice to see you, Ginger."

"Never mind nice-to-see-me nonsense," said Ginger. "You is scarin' Ginger's scoggins away."

"Not *all* of it," said Maxwell, pushing the bag towards him.

Ginger sniffed hopefully.

"Is bag full of ratses?"

"Have a look and see."

Ginger stuck his head into the bag, snuffling and mewling as he chewed through the rest of the pasty. After a while, he pulled his head out and stared at Maxwell.

"Why you giving me this?"

"Because you were hungry."

Ginger licked gravy from his whiskers. "Dogs is daft," he said. "Barky-barky, bossin' us about."

"Speaking of which," said Maxwell, "you should probably go now."

Ginger pricked up his ears and nodded.

"You not so bad for a dog," he said.

Then he slunk off into the shadows.

Seconds later, Mr B and Restreppo came bounding from the bushes. "Maxwell, we've been looking for you everywhere!" barked Mr B. "Madison's gone off in a huff and Restreppo's depressed."

"Why?" asked Maxwell. He glanced at Restreppo and saw that his lower lip was wobbling. "What's the matter?"

"I don't want to talk about it," said Restreppo.

"Fair enough."

"Except that I do!" sobbed Restreppo, lying down and putting his paws over his eyes. "Officer Marshall is a big stupid meany and that's all there is to it!"

"Restreppo saw some photos," explained Mr B. "On Officer Marshall's desk."

"What kind of photos?"

"PHOTOS OF OTHER DOGS!"

cried Restreppo.

"Younger ones! Prettier ones!

Some were even wearing fancy *bows*!"

"Restreppo's worried he's got too old," whispered

Mr B. "He thinks Officer Marshall wants to get rid

of him and get a new dog instead."

"He *does* want to get rid of me!" whimpered

Restreppo. "I know he does!"

"You don't *know* that, Restreppo."

"Why else would he be looking at photos of other dogs? Solving crimes with him was my thing and now I can't do it any more."

"Why don't you come with me?" said Maxwell. "You could help me find my friend."

"No!" cried Restreppo, thumping the ground with his paw. "I'm just going to stay here and die!"

"I think he's a bit upset," said Mr B.

"Come on, Restreppo," said Maxwell. "Everyone knows what a good police dog you are."

Restreppo sat up and wiped his eyes with the back of his paw. "I *am* a good police dog!"

"And let's face it," added Mr B, "with all those new dog pictures to look at, Officer Marshall's not going to miss you for a while."

"That's not even funny," said Restreppo.

"Come on, what do you say?" asked Maxwell.

"Are you ready to show Officer Marshall you've still got what it takes?"

Restreppo sat up straight and snapped a police-dog-paw salute against the side of his head.

"POLICE DOG RESTREPPO NUMBER FOUR-FIVE-SIX, REPORTING FOR DUTY, SAH!"

CHAPTER SEVEN
Crossing The Bridge

"If the sound's coming from the other side of the city then we'll need to cross the bridge," said Restreppo. "It's not far from here."

Maxwell followed Restreppo and Mr B through a twist of narrow streets until they came to a road which opened out towards a long, sweeping bridge. On either side of the bridge were thin strips of pavement with stone balustrades running alongside them. When they reached the pavement, Maxwell stopped. He remembered the musty smell of the sack,

the dark churning water and
the snap of Paisley's collar
as she was torn away by the
current.

"Everything all right?" asked Restreppo.

"I know this place," said Maxwell. "This is where
they threw me in."

Mr B sat beside him and stared at the river below.
"Don't worry," he said. "*We're* here now."

Maxwell breathed in and tasted the smell of the
river on the wind. **"i DON'T THiNK i CAN DO iT,"**
he said. "I don't think I can cross over."

"Of course you can," said Mr B. "Hey, Restreppo.
Get over here."

Restreppo wandered over and sat on the other
side of Maxwell. As the dogs huddled up close,
Maxwell felt their warmth and for a moment he felt
safe again.

"Officer Marshall and I used to drive across this bridge all the time," said Restreppo. "I used to lick the window and everything."

Maxwell stared at the city lights reflected in the water. "I think what Restreppo's trying to say," said Mr B, "is that we're your friends and we promise we won't let bad things happen to you."

"That's it," said Restreppo. He thought for a moment. "Licking windows is fun."

Mr B turned to Maxwell. "OK?"

Maxwell nodded. "I think so."

"In that case ... lead the way."

Maxwell took one last look at the river and set off across the bridge, watching the lights of cars and lorries flash past.

"DON'T LOOK DOWN!" shouted Mr B. "Just keep your eyes ahead!"

They were nearly halfway across the bridge when a white van skidded to a halt in front of them and two men jumped out.

Maxwell saw that one of the men was wearing jeans and a yellow scarf beneath a leather jacket.

On his head he wore a cowboy hat.

"Well, look what we have here," he said as the traffic rumbled past. "A bunch of dogs in search of a home. How about you all come on over and say hello to your Uncle Dabsley?"

"Look, Mr B!" barked Restreppo. "A dog's best friend has come to help us!"

"WAIT!" barked Maxwell as Restreppo and Mr B ran towards Dabsley.

But his warning was lost in the whirr of traffic and as his friends jumped up to lick the men's hands, Maxwell realized that Dabsley and Ferris weren't interested in him at all.

It was Restreppo and Mr B they were after.

Maxwell ducked down behind the van and tried to attract his friends' attention.

"RESTREPPO!" he shouted. **"MR B!"**

But both dogs were so busy being fussed over that they didn't notice.

Maxwell was about to run around the other side of the van when he heard a muffled voice shout, "Hey kid! In here!"

Maxwell looked up and was surprised to see Madison scowling out of the back window.

"QUICK! LET ME OUT!"

Maxwell jumped up at the door, bounced off and fell to the ground. Then, remembering how Paisley had opened the cupboard for him, he leapt up again and his teeth grazed the edge of the door handle.

"That's it, kid!" barked Madison. "Tear that handle right off!"

Maxwell backed up a few paces, took a deep breath and hurled himself at the van.

There was a thud as he hit the door, but this time he clamped his teeth around the handle and the door swung open.

"Nice work," said Madison. He checked his reflection in the window and turned to look at Maxwell, who was still hanging on to the handle by his teeth.

"OK, kid. You can let go now."

Maxwell fell to the ground and Madison jumped down next to him.

"I'm confused," he said. "One minute I'm taking a whiz, the next I'm banged up in a van. What's going on?"

"See for yourself," said Maxwell.

Madison peered round the wheel just as Dabsley grabbed Restreppo and threw him in the front of the van. Before he could protest, Ferris picked up Mr B and pushed him in too.

"Wow," said Madison. "Who *are* those guys?"

"The same ones who threw me and Paisley in the river."

"Seriously?"

Maxwell nodded.

"So they like throwing dogs around," said Madison. "What are we going to do about it?"

Maxwell growled.

"Sounds good," said Madison. "Anything else?"

Maxwell bared his teeth.

"OK, now you're talking my language..."

Maxwell barked twice, ground his teeth together and snarled.

"My thoughts exactly!" shouted Madison.

"OK, KID, LET'S GO!"

With an angry bark he ran straight at Ferris, leapt up and knocked him to the ground.

"HELP!" screeched Ferris. **"THERE'S A POODLE ON MY FACE!"**

Maxwell threw himself at Dabsley and bit his ankle before dodging a kick and leaping up onto the driver's seat. Mr B was in the foot well tidying up sweet wrappers and Restreppo was staring out of the window whispering, "I'm trying to be good, Officer Marshall. I'm *trying* to be good."

"These are the men who tried to drown me!" shouted Maxwell. "We have to get out of here!"

Before Restreppo could reply, Madison flew past him and hit the passenger window, sliding down the glass into the foot well next to Mr B.

"Madison," said Mr B. "What a lovely surprise."

Dabsley reached in and grabbed Maxwell in his fist.

"You and me got some unfinished business," he said.

Maxwell barked and snapped and twisted in Dabsley's hands, but Dabsley held him fast as he strode to the edge of the bridge, where he held Maxwell out over the river.

"Say goodbye, Mutt," he said.

"Please!" whimpered Maxwell, watching the dark water swirl beneath him. "Don't throw me in again!"

But Dabsley just smiled. "No one wants you," he said. "This is what happens when you mess with me."

Dabsley's muscles tensed and Maxwell knew that the world would soon be lost.

But as he closed his eyes there was a shout, and when he opened them again he was lying on the ground. Above him, Restreppo and Madison clung to the sides of Dabsley's jacket while Mr B swung from the front like a pendulum.

"Ferris, come and help me out!" yelled Dabsley, punching at the dogs with his fists. "They're killing me over here!"

"We haven't even started," growled Madison.

"I don't sink I can hold on nuch nonger," said Mr B through gritted teeth.

The three dogs dropped to the ground and Madison spat out a piece of Dabsley's jacket.

Maxwell shook himself and got to his feet.

"You OK, big dog?" asked Madison.

"I think so," said Maxwell.

"Then let's go," said Restreppo.

As they ran towards the lights of the city, Maxwell heard Dabsley shouting, "If I ever see you again you're dead dogs, do you hear me? **DEAD DOGS!**"

But all Maxwell could think about was how his friends had kept their promise, and how he had been unable to do the same for Paisley.

CHAPTER EIGHT
LOOKING FOR CLUES

"That was *dreadful!*" gasped Mr B when they reached the backstreets on the other side of the bridge. "I feel completely *traumatized!*"

"I don't know why you get so emotional," said Madison. "It was a fight and we won it. End of story."

"But Maxwell could have *died!*"

"Yeah, but he didn't."

Mr B sighed. "I don't understand you, Madison. Don't you ever feel any emotion?"

Madison shook his head. "Can't be doing with it."

"Mr B's right though," said Restreppo. "We nearly lost Maxwell back there. This whole thing is getting far too dangerous."

Maxwell leaned against the soot-stained wall and listened to the sounds of the city coming alive. "It's not me they're after," he said. "It's you."

Restreppo frowned. "Why do you say that?"

"Before Dabsley threw us in the river, he said he didn't want us because we weren't on the cards. So if he wants you, then maybe you *are* on the cards. Whatever that means."

"Wait," said Madison. "When I was in the van I heard them talk about some crazy red-haired lady who lives in a big house by the lake. They called her The Collector."

"That's who Dachshund Dan was talking about!"

gasped Mr B. "The one who chops dogs' heads off and sticks them on the wall!"

"You know what?" said Madison. "If it shuts you up, I'm all for it."

The clouds blushed a deep pink as the morning sun cast its light across the city.

Maxwell listened to the clatter of shops and factories opening their doors to a new day. Somewhere, mixed in with the noise of the city and the song of the wind, he thought he heard the sound again.

But then it was gone, leaving only a faint echo on the morning breeze.

"You still hear it, don't you?" asked Restreppo.

Maxwell nodded.

"Sometimes."

"You think it's important?"

69

"Yes. But I don't know why."

"Maybe not knowing doesn't matter," said Restreppo. "I don't know why Officer Marshall is being mean, but it made me come along with you. So maybe it's the looking that matters. Maybe the knowing comes later."

"Restreppo's right," said Mr B. "We might not know what we're doing, but we know we want to help."

"Even if it's dangerous?" asked Maxwell.

"*Especially* if it's dangerous," said Madison.

Maxwell set off across the road, comforted by the fact that his friends were with him. He guessed Ridley was right, that sometimes looking for one thing could lead to finding another. But he was still worried he might be leading his friends into danger.

And for what?

For the sake of some strange sound that might be no more than his imagination.

Running through a series of alleyways, he stopped beside some dustbins overflowing with rubbish. As the others skidded round the corner behind him, Maxwell realized two things: firstly, that a group of dogs were staring at them from the middle of the alley and secondly, it was not only good things that happened unexpectedly.

CHAPTER NINE
The East Street dogs

"WELL, WELL, WELL," growled a large Dobermann, baring her teeth. "What have we here?"

"What we have," said Madison, "is four dogs looking for a fight."

"Oh yeah?" said the Dobermann. "You think you can mess with us?"

"Certainly do," said Madison, squeezing his paws until they cracked. **"WHO'S FIRST?"**

"Leave it, Madison," said Restreppo as two spaniels, a bull terrier and a fierce-looking Rottweiler lined up behind the Dobermann.

"Maybe I'll just tidy up a bit," said Mr B, running
over to the bins and arranging the rubbish into
piles. "Restreppo? Do you want to give me a hand
over here?"

"Come on," said Madison, "I'll take you all on."

"Don't listen to him," called Mr B. "It's his
haircut. It's done strange things to his head."

"I'll do strange things to *his* head in a minute,"
growled the Dobermann.

Maxwell knew it was his fault that his friends were here. So he walked towards the snarling Dobermann and tried to ignore the fear that fluttered around his heart.

"How are you?" he said.

"Have you had a nice day?"

The Dobermann stared at him and laughed. "He's asking how we are!" she said, turning to the other dogs. "He's asking if we've had a nice day!"

"We have actually," said the bull terrier. "What with the sun out and everything, it's been just lovely."

The Dobermann gave him a look. "Dave, what have we talked about?"

"I don't know."

"Yes you do. Yes. You. Do. What have we said about you being over-friendly to dogs you don't know?"

"Oh, *that*," said Dave. "Sorry, Darlene."

"Darlene?" said Mr B. He stopped piling up potatoes and pressed a paw to his chest. "That is *such* a lovely name."

"It is a lovely name, isn't it?" agreed Dave. "I've always said so."

"Look, just forget about my name," growled Darlene. "Who do you think you are, coming into our alley like this?"

"We're not here to cause trouble," said Maxwell.

"Speak for yourself," said Madison, thumping his paws together.

"You're already causing trouble," said Darlene. "And if you stay here a minute longer, trouble's going to come snarling down the street to get you."

"Metaphorically speaking of course," said Dave.

"Shut it, Dave," said Darlene. "Now either you dogs get back to where you came from, or me and my friends are going to teach you a lesson. Aren't we, lads?"

"We sure is," growled the other dogs.

"We sure *are*," said Dave. "Plural."

"Well, we *could* go home," said Madison. "Or we could stay and give you puppies something to howl about."

Darlene pushed Maxwell out of the way and squared up to Madison.

"You think you can take on the East Street Dogs? You and your powder-puff hair?"

"I don't *think* so," said Madison, "I *know* so."

"Oh you do, do you?"

"Yeah," said Madison, primping his hair with one paw. "I poodly-do."

"YOU OTHER DOGS, KEEP BACK!" barked

Restreppo.

"You gonna make us?" snarled the Rottweiler.

"I don't know," said Restreppo, baring his teeth.
"Are you gonna *make* us make you?"

"That depends. Are you going to *make* us make
you make us?"

"PLEASE!" cried Mr B, pressing his paws over his
ears. "Won't somebody stop this madness?"

As the dogs jostled and growled at one another,
Maxwell knew it was only a matter of time before
a fight started. Catching sight of an old cabbage
next to the bins, a memory flashed through
his mind.

"STOP!" he shouted,
running over and
nudging the cabbage
with his nose.

"Come and see what I found!"

Darlene and Madison stopped pushing each other and turned to look at Maxwell.

The two spaniels – Dibber and Dobber – glanced at each other and coughed awkwardly.

"It's ... a cabbage," said Darlene.

"Exactly," said Maxwell. "Watch this."

Putting his paw beneath the cabbage, he flicked it up into the air. The cabbage spun across the alley, bounced in the dirt and rolled to a stop in front of Darlene.

"WOAH!" said Darlene, taking a step back. "What's your game?"

"It's not *my* game," said Maxwell. "It's everyone's game. It's called football."

"Never heard of it," said Darlene. "What's it for?"

"Fun," said Maxwell. "Kick it back to me."

"Why?"

"Just try it."

Darlene looked at the Rottweiler.

"What d'you reckon, Rodge?"

Rodge shrugged.

"Might be a laugh."

Darlene tapped the cabbage with the back of her paw and watched it roll forward.

"HEY!" she shouted. "Hey everyone! Did you see me do that?"

"Kick it again," said Maxwell, rolling it back. "Kick it harder."

This time Darlene took a run up and walloped it across the alley. The cabbage sailed through the air, bounced twice and hit the bins with a clang.

"TRASHED iT!" shouted Darlene as the other dogs cheered. "Ding-dong and in the dustbin!"

"That really was awfully good," said Dave.

"I want a go," said Madison.

"And me," said Rodge.

"And me, and me, and me!" chorused the others.

"We can all have a go," said Maxwell. "That's what's so great about it."

"But we've only got one cabbage," said Darlene, who already seemed to have forgotten about the fight.

"We just need two teams," explained Maxwell. "Then we try and score in each other's goals."

As the dogs gathered round excitedly, Maxwell remembered what Ridley had said.

In between the looking, there's always fun to be had.

CHAPTER TEN

Taking Sides

"These are the goals," explained Maxwell, dropping two potatoes at either end of the alley. "One team is at *this* end and the other team is at *that* end. The idea is to kick the cabbage between the posts of the other team's goal. The one who scores the most is the winner."

"That's it?" asked Rodge.

"That's it."

"Genius," said Dave.

"You can say that again," whispered Mr B. "Maxwell's turned fighting into football."

"Never mind," said Madison. "We can always turn it back again."

"Let's mix the teams up," said Maxwell. "Mr B, you can be one captain and Dave, you can be the other."

"i'M A CAPTAiN, i'M A CAPTAiN!" cried Dave, skipping round in a circle. "Wait. What's a captain?"

"You just need to pick someone."

"OK. I pick the bulldog."

"You can't," said Rodge. "He's the other captain."

"Oh, listen to me, what am I like?" said Dave. "In that case I choose ... the mouthy one."

"Who are you calling mouthy?" said Madison.

"You, because you are," said Mr B.

Madison nodded. "Fair enough."

"My turn," said Mr B. "I choose ... Rodge."

"Me?" said Rodge, pointing at himself. "That is *so* nice of you!"

"Come on, Rodge, toughen up a bit," said Darlene. "We're supposed to be a gang, for goodness' sake."

"Oh, so we can't have manners now, is that it?" said Rodge.

Darlene looked at Madison. "You see what I have to put up with?"

"Tell me about it," said Madison.

"Let's make a start," said Maxwell, dribbling the cabbage to the middle of the alley. Dibber and Dobber ran to their goals, then Maxwell shouted **"PEEP!"** and passed the cabbage back to Madison. Rodge ran towards it but Madison flicked the cabbage through his legs and ran past him.

"Hey, where'd that go?" said Rodge.

"OVER, HERE!" shouted Maxwell.

Madison did a little step-over, sent Restreppo the wrong way and flicked the cabbage up in the air. Maxwell threw himself forward and headed it so hard that it splattered against the wall.

"GET iN!" cried Darlene, running round the dustbins. "Have some of that!"

"All right, don't wet yourself," said Rodge sulkily. "You haven't won yet."

He kicked the cabbage to Restreppo, who knocked it to Mr B. Mr B passed it back to Restreppo, who sent Darlene the wrong way before spinning round, flicking it past Dobber and barking, "Thank you and goodnight!"

Rodge and Mr B stood side by side, waving their paws and chanting,

"THOSE DOGS! THOSE DOGS! THOSE DOGS ARE GOING DOWN!"

"Don't listen to them," said Maxwell. "We can still win."

He rolled the cabbage to Dave, who pawed it back to Madison. Madison stuck his front paw underneath and flipped it high over the heads of the other dogs. As the cabbage spun through the air Maxwell stood on his hind legs, cushioned it on his chest and flicked it into Darlene's path.

"Hit it, Darlene!" he shouted. **"HiT iT!"**

With an excited yelp, Darlene caught it on the volley but her legs slipped out from under her and she hoofed it over her shoulder. It smacked Madison on the head and flew into the goal.

"SHE SCORED!" shouted Rodge as Madison fell over. **"iN HER OWN GOAL!"**

"Oops," said Darlene.

Dibber giggled.

Dobber sniggered.

Then Madison got up, went cross-eyed
and fell over again.

Darlene snorted so hard that she got
hiccups and Rodge had to slap her on
the back to calm her down.

"YOWCH!" yelped Darlene, which
made everyone laugh even more, especially when
Mr B tried to do an impression of Darlene and
banged his head on a dustbin.

"This is the best day ever," said Darlene when
everyone had finally calmed down. "Who knew
cabbages could be so much fun?"

The sun went behind a cloud and Maxwell
shivered. "It's been lovely meeting you all," he
said, "but I think I should get going now. I made
a promise, you see, and I need to keep it."

"What kind of promise?" asked Darlene.

"I promised to look after my friend Paisley,"

said Maxwell, "but I lost her in the river."

"She's a girl?" said Darlene.

Maxwell nodded. "Well, I can understand why you're worried," said Darlene. "But in my experience, girls are pretty good at looking after themselves."

"The thing is, she helped me when I was in trouble," said Maxwell. "She told me that friends never give up."

Darlene looked at him. "*Have* you given up?"

"No."

"Then I can't see the problem," said Darlene.

At that moment a woman's voice floated softly down the alleyway.

"HELLO MY FRiENDS!" she called. "Come and see what lovely things I've got for you!"

"Did she say *lovely things?*" asked Mr B.

"I think she did," said Dave.

"But I *love* lovely things!"

"Me too! The thing I always say about lovely things is that they're always so *lovely*!"

"You hit the nail on the head there, Dave."

"Wait a minute," said Maxwell, who had already learned enough about the world to know that things were not always as they seemed. "I think we should be careful."

"COO-EE, LiTTLE DOGGiES," called the voice. "Come and see what I've got for you!"

A woman appeared at the bottom of the alleyway clutching two carrier bags. Her trousers were tucked into a pair of green wellingtons and although the day was warm she wore a padded coat over a purple jumper. Around her neck was a string of pearls and she wore a silk scarf over her head, knotted beneath the chin.

Darlene sniffed the air. "Does anyone smell what I smell?"

"If that ain't meat," said Rodge, "then I'm a mouse called Mary."

The woman upended the carrier bags and a pile of shiny red lumps fell to the ground.

"It *is* meat!" cried Dave.

"MEEEATT!" shouted Madison.

"Wait," said Restreppo, sniffing the air. "Maxwell is right. We need to be careful." He looked around. "Anyone got any thoughts?"

Madison held his paw in the air. "I have."

"Go on."

"It's meat."

"Good point," said Rodge. "Anyone else?"

"Umm ... it's *meat*," said Dave.

"Fair enough," said Mr B. "Can't see any holes in that argument."

"Good," said Restreppo. "Glad we discussed it."

"OK!" shouted Rodge. **"LET'S GO GET SOME!"**

As the dogs charged down the alley, a delicious smell drifted into Maxwell's nostrils and before he knew it he was running after the others, unable to stop himself.

"That's it, my lovelies!" cooed the woman. "Take your time! There's enough here for everyone!"

It was only when Maxwell was chewing the last chunk of meat that he noticed the day start to wobble at the edges. He staggered sideways and stared through a misty haze to see the others lying in a heap.

"Time for a nap, I think," yawned Restreppo.

"You can say that again," said Dave.

"Actually, I don't think I can," said Restreppo. He put his head on his paws and started to snore.

"Maybe I'll just tidy up a bit," said Mr B. He picked up a carrier bag, then fell over with the bag still clutched in his teeth.

"Something's wrong," said Maxwell, trying to keep the world in focus. "She's put something in the meat. We have to..."

But the words wouldn't come.

"QUICKLY!" shouted the woman, clapping her hands together. "We've got them!"

A white van reversed around the corner and two men jumped out. Maxwell looked back at the woman and saw a wisp of red hair escape from the edge of her scarf.

They work for her, he thought as Dabsley and Ferris wrenched the van doors open and threw his friends in one by one. *The Collector has come and it's all my fault.*

"This one was never on the cards, m'lady," said Dabsley, grabbing Maxwell by the scruff of the neck. "This one ain't nothing but trouble."

"Then get rid of him," said the woman.

"It'll be my pleasure," said Dabsley.

With a grunt, he drew back his arm and hurled Maxwell down the alley. As Maxwell's world turned upside down there was a thump and a clang.

In the distance, he heard the slamming of doors.

Then everything went black.

CHAPTER ELEVEN

LOST aNd FOUNd

It was dark when Maxwell opened his eyes.

Peering into the gloom, he heard a faint tapping noise.

"Hello?" said Maxwell. "Who's there?"

"Ah-ha," said a voice. "The dog's a-waking hi'self up."

Maxwell was sitting in a dustbin, surrounded by old newspapers and vegetable peelings. Above him, the sky was bright with stars.

"How did I get in here?" he asked.

"The big man throwed you in, smash-bash-crash."

Maxwell frowned. "Ginger, is that you?"

"Is me, yes," replied Ginger, his face appearing at the top of the dustbin. Maxwell felt the world tip, then the dustbin toppled over with a clang. He staggered out, splashed through a puddle and shook himself.

"LOOK OUT, Y'LITTLE YAPSTER!" yelled Ginger, taking cover behind the dustbin. "Don't be washin' me with weather-water!"

"Sorry about that," said Maxwell. "But what are you doing here? I thought you lived on the other side of the river."

"Ginger lives where he wants," said Ginger, wiping water from his whiskers. He pushed a collar with a gold tag on it towards Maxwell. "Looky-looky."

"This is Paisley's collar," said Maxwell. "Where did you find it?"

"You's leavin' it by Ginger's binser. But you give Ginger scoggins, so Ginger's bringin' it back again."

He pulled out one of his whiskers and used it to fix the collar around Maxwell's neck.

"As well as speakin' good, I is also practical," he said. "So maybe now you is findin' Paisley too."

Maxwell shook his head. "I thought I was getting close, but then I lost all my friends."

"*Oh, poor me, I is lost all my friends,*" said Ginger. "So who is this, then, I is wonderin'?" He pointed at himself and Maxwell frowned.

"Ginger, are you my friend?"

"Well, I is not a panful of pizza," said Ginger. "So now I is thinkin' you must be doing what you does best. And I's not talking 'bout scoggins-stealin' neither. Ginger's talking 'bout *listenin'*."

As Ginger flicked water from his fur, Maxwell realized he had completely forgotten about the sound. So he sat back on his haunches, lifted his ears and listened. He heard the dripping of raindrops, the clatter of cars, the whisper of the wind and the beating of his heart. It was as if all the sounds of the city were tangled up together:

phones ringing, dogs barking, babies crying, birds chattering...

"Is you hearin' anything?" asked Ginger.

"Not yet."

"Then do more listenin'."

Maxwell listened again. This time he heard the cry of a kestrel, the rattle of trucks and the jangle of coins. And then, buried beneath all of these things, he heard something so small and quiet that he almost missed it.

"Oh," said Maxwell. "There it is."

It was the sound he had heard before.

It was the sound of someone singing.

CHAPTER TWELVE

Rosie Morello

"You know this place?" asked Ginger as they stood

in a moonlit park next to some rusty swings.

"I think so," said Maxwell. Tufts of grass pushed

their way through cracks in the concrete and fingers of bindweed twisted up the fence.

He remembered how when Paisley had freed him from the dark cupboard, he had peered through a crack in the curtains and seen the same abandoned play-park. Now he looked up at the block of flats and listened to the sound of singing floating through an open window.

"That's the sound I used to hear," he said. "This is where I used to live."

As they made their way up the concrete steps, Maxwell's heart was filled with hope.

Could Paisley have found her way back here too?

Reaching the top of the steps, Maxwell walked slowly down the corridor towards the sound of the singing. As he got nearer, he passed a half-open door and caught the scent of dust slowly settling.

He turned his head and saw the closed curtains, the tatty red sofa and the frayed rug on the floor. He knew at once that it was the place where he had huddled in the corner with Paisley, hiding from the man who had shouted and threatened and thrown them into the river.

But now Dabsley was gone and only the faintest scent of him remained.

"**PAISLEY!**" he barked. "Where are you?"

"Don't want to be sayin' it," said Ginger, "but this place seems empty of all dogs except you."

"She *has* to be here," said Maxwell.

But as the lady next door sang her sad, beautiful song, he stared into the empty cupboard and knew his friend was never coming back.

And so Maxwell Mutt sat down on the rug and threw back his head and howled.

"Who is making all this fuss and interrupting

Rosie Morello's singing?"

A large woman wearing fluffy
pink slippers and a blue silk
kimono stood in the doorway.
Her hair was swept up into a bun
held neatly in place by two shiny
chopsticks. In her hands she held
a tin containing a freshly baked
chocolate cake.

"Yes, that's me: Rosie Morello –
cleaner, animal-lover and would-be opera singer!"

Maxwell watched as she put the cake down,
flung her arms open and spun around on one foot.
Despite her size, she danced so lightly it was as if
she weighed nothing at all.

"Why so sad, little dog?" she asked, bending
down and stroking his head. "Have you lost
someone, like me?"

Maxwell stared at the dusty curtains and said nothing.

"I thought perhaps you were one of the little dogs who lived here before. But that cruel man never kept them for long. He was so rude, my dears! He kept telling me he was too good for this place and that he was going to live with Lady Pinkerton in the house by the lake. But he is mad, I think."

Rosie crossed to the window and peered through the curtains into the night. "He couldn't even pay his rent for this place and now he is gone," she said, shaking her head. "Good riddance, I say! I shall not weep for him. But now my little one is gone too, and I shall weep for her until the very end of time!"

Rosie covered her face and sobbed.

Although Maxwell understood her sadness, he

wasn't ready to give up yet. **"PAISLEY!"** he shouted.
"WHERE ARE YOU? IT'S ME – MAXWELL!"

"Shush, little dog," said Rosie, drying her eyes and patting his head. "I know this world can be a dark and lonely place. But somehow we have to find a way to let in the light."

She pulled back the curtains and a shaft of moonlight shone across the carpet.

Then she began to sing.

"*Ninna nanna, ninna oh,*
Questo bimbo a chi lo do?
Ninna nanna, ninna oh,
Questo bimbo me lo terrò." *

As the notes swirled around him, Maxwell was so overcome that he threw back his head and howled once more.

* *Lullaby, lullaby, ooh,*
Who will I give this baby to?
Lullaby, lullaby-ee,
I will keep this baby for me.

Ginger watched him for a moment, then cleared his throat and began to yowl, straining his neck in an effort to reach the high notes.

"That's it, my little friends!" cried Rosie. "Sing until your voices become angels!"

She wandered across the hallway to her own flat and as Maxwell followed he saw that every space on her living room shelves was filled with china animals: dogs, cats, rabbits and birds; even a small pottery pig next to a mouse staring up at the moon.

"Meet my other animal friends," said Rosie,

spreading her arms wide. "They might not be real like you, but I love them just the same."

"She crazy," said Ginger as Rosie began to sing again.

"No she's not," said Maxwell. "She's lonely."

Suddenly, Rosie Morello stopped singing.

Ginger snapped his mouth shut and the clack of his teeth echoed around the room.

"Don't nook now," he said, his teeth still clenched, "but I shink she's shtaring at you."

"Come here, little dog," said Rosie.

She knelt down and peered at the disc around Maxwell's neck. "Where did you get this?"

Maxwell saw a flash of anger in her eyes and it reminded him of the look on Dabsley's face before he'd thrown him in the cupboard.

"NO!" he yelped, backing into a corner. "Go away!"

"Hush now," said Rosie, kneeling in front of him. "I didn't mean to scare you. But you're wearing something that belongs to me."

"It's not yours!" barked Maxwell. "It's Paisley's!"

"Stop yer yappin'," said Ginger, covering his ears. "Is achin' my head."

"I just want to know where my Paisley has gone," said Rosie. "Is that too much to ask?"

"MAXWELL!" hissed Ginger, taking his paws away from his ears. "Is you hearin' what she's sayin'? She is sayin' the name Paisley!"

As Maxwell stared out of the window he saw, nestling in some trees towards the outskirts of the city, a brightly lit house reflected in a pool of water. He thought of Dabsley and The Collector, and of what Rosie had said about the house by the lake, and his heart began to beat faster.

"**THERE iT iS!**" he shouted, jumping up and scrabbling at the window with his paws. "That's the house by the lake! That's where she must have taken them!"

"Now, now, little dog, no need to get excited," said Rosie Morello. "There will be plenty of time for a walk in the morning."

"iT'S THE HOUSE, iT'S THE HOUSE!" barked Maxwell, jumping up at the glass, but Rosie just shook her head and moved him away from the window.

"Why don't we play a game?" she said, settling herself on the sofa. "I know. Let's play a game of lying still and seeing who can be the quietest."

"Ooh, is my kind of game," said Ginger, curling up next to her.

Suddenly Maxwell remembered the sounds game he had played with Royston and Ridley. **"i'VE GOT iT!"** he said, running around the room. "Sounds like..."

Ginger sat up and stared at him.

"Now you is talkin' crazy."

Maxwell ignored him and pawed at the carpet.

"What's the matter, little doggy?" asked Rosie, leaning forward. "Are you trying to tell me something?"

Maxwell wagged his tail and leapt up onto the arm of the sofa. Then he grabbed the pottery pig, the china mouse and the figure of a shepherdess in his mouth.

"Hey!" said Rosie. "Be careful with those!"

Maxwell jumped down and placed them on the carpet, touching each one in turn with his nose.

"Ooh, is this a guessing game?" asked Rosie, clapping her hands together. "I *love* guessing games!"

Maxwell nudged the figures again and looked up at her.

"Pig, mouse, girl," said Rosie. "Is that it?"

Maxwell barked twice, snapped his teeth next to the china shepherdess, then looked at Rosie.

"Lamb?" said Rosie.

Maxwell whined.

"Shepherdess?"

Maxwell whined once more,

then snapped his teeth beside the girl again.

"You're ... trying to *bite* her?"

Maxwell barked, then ran back to the two figures and nudged them with his nose.

"Pig, mouse, biter," said Rosie.

Maxwell leapt up beside the cake and barked.

"I don't think chocolate cake is good for small dogs' tummies," said Rosie.

"Is good for catses'," said Ginger.

"Shush, kitty."

Maxwell barked again.

"Pig, mouse, biter ... cake! But what does it mean?"

"Means all dogs is crazy," said Ginger.

"I give up," sighed Maxwell.

Ginger stared out of the window and his eyes widened. "Wait. Pig, mouse, biter, cake. Is you sayin' *big house by the lake?*"

"Yes!" said Maxwell. He frowned. "How did you know?"

"I is watchin' the ratses play that game," said Ginger. "But why's you tellin' her about the house?"

"Because Dabsley called The Collector m'lady and Rosie said he's gone to live in the big house with Lady Pinkerton."

"So?"

"So The Collector and Lady Pinkerton must be the same person!"

"The one what collects dogses?" said Ginger, staring at the house.

"Not only that," said Maxwell, running towards the door. "If Dachshund Dan's right then we have to move fast before she starts chopping their heads off."

He stopped in the hallway. "Please, Rosie," he said, "help us find Paisley."

But Rosie just looked confused. "I don't understand," she said. "Why would a mouse bite a cake?"

"'Cos he *hungry*," said Ginger, staring at the cake.

"Ginger, forget the cake," said Maxwell. **"WE HAVE TO GO NOW!"**

Together they ran down the stairs and into the street. As they hurried past the pubs and cafes and sandwich shops and flower stalls, Maxwell heard the sound of Rosie's voice still trilling in his ears:

"Wait for me, little dog! Please don't go!"

CHAPTER THIRTEEN

The house By The Lake

The moon hung low in the treetops as Maxwell led the way up a narrow lane towards the gates of the big house. The breeze ruffled his fur and he smelled wild garlic in the air; as they emerged from the tree-covered lane he looked back and saw the river shimmering in the distance.

"What you seein', yapster?" asked Ginger.

"The river," said Maxwell. "I never realized it looked so beautiful."

"How things are lookin' depends on where you is standin'," said Ginger. "And from where I's standin' you's lookin' scarified."

Maxwell stared at the silhouette of the house and realized he was shaking.

"Park yer paws, pupkin. We can walk backaways if you wants."

"No," said Maxwell. "I'm not giving up now."

Ginger stared at him in the moonlight. "You is brave dog," he said.

"I don't feel it," said Maxwell.

"Then you is double-brave." With a flick of his legs, Ginger leapt up the wall and sat next to the gate. "Stayin' down or comin' up?"

Maxwell dug his claws between the bricks, but the mortar crumbled and he fell back with a yelp.

"Shhh!" hissed Ginger. "No more yowlin'!"

He jumped down and stretched himself against the wall. "Look. Ginger is bein' a cat ladder."

Maxwell looked at him doubtfully. "Are you sure? I don't want to hurt you."

"Pfff, I is fine," said Ginger. "Just don't be stampin' on me noober."

Maxwell took a running jump, bounced off Ginger's head and sprang up onto the wall.

"AWWW," shouted Ginger, clutching his head. **"NOOBER, STAMP."**

"Sorry about that," said Maxwell. He stretched out a paw. "Here, let me help you up."

Ginger looked at him disdainfully. "I is a cat, you spaggins. Cats don't need no helpin'."

He sprang neatly on top of the wall, then together they jumped down and ran to where the light from the windows cast deep shadows across the lawn.

As they crouched in the bushes, Maxwell peered through the window and saw Lady Pinkerton talking to Dabsley. Above the fireplace, two silver axes were fixed to the wall. On either side of them were two glass display cases.

Maxwell crept closer and listened.

"Look around you, Mr Dabsley," Lady Pinkerton was saying. "What do you see on the walls?"

Dabsley shrugged. "A couple of axes and a bunch of bugs."

"Those are not bugs, Mr Dabsley.
They are butterflies. Just some of
the many beautiful specimens I
have collected over the years."

Ginger nudged Maxwell. "Why's
she collectin' dead stuff?"

"I don't know." Maxwell shivered
and wondered what had become of
his friends.

"I provided you with a place to live, Mr Dabsley,"
continued Lady Pinkerton. "All I asked in return
was that you found me the exact species of dogs
I wanted and built me a gallery to display them.
Have you done either of those things?"

"Just give me a few more days," said Dabsley.
"We got some dogs today, didn't we?"

"Yes we did," replied Lady Pinkerton, "and the
only reason we got them is because *I* came along

and got them for you. You're a waste of space, Mr Dabsley. So I suggest you and your friend pack up your things and get off my property immediately."

"You're throwing me out?" asked Dabsley. "After all I've done for you?"

"I don't need you, Mr Dabsley," replied Lady Pinkerton. "In fact I don't need anyone. Life is much easier when you're alone."

Dabsley's face grew redder by the second. Sweat beaded beneath the brim of his cowboy hat and he stared wildly around the room, clenching his fists as if he wanted to punch someone.

"You want me to go?" he said. "Fine, I'll go. But first I'm going to pay one last visit to your precious collection."

"I think he's talkin' about the dogses," whispered Ginger.

"DON'T YOU DARE HARM THEM!" cried
Lady Pinkerton, her hands trembling. **"LEAVE
THEM ALONE!"**

"He is very bad mankin," said Ginger.

Dabsley smiled, revealing a row of yellowing
teeth. Then he ripped an axe off the wall so hard
that bits of plaster pattered onto the carpet.

"I could take 'em down to the river, same as I did
with the others," he said. "But it's late and I'm tired.
So maybe I'll just finish 'em off right here."

"STOP!" cried Lady Pinkerton **"i FORBiD iT!"**

"She flibbids it!" shouted Ginger, jumping around
in the shrubbery. "She flibbids it, she flibbids it!"

"Shhh, they'll hear you!" said Maxwell, putting
his paw over Ginger's mouth.

"Aw cawn't breef," said Ginger. Then, when
Maxwell took his paw away, he added, "I's havin'
a idea," and whispered it in Maxwell's ear.

121

"I can't do that," said Maxwell. "You'll be killed!"

"Pfff, you's thinkin' of dogses," said Ginger. "Cats is havin' nine lives, remember?"

Maxwell looked at Dabsley through the window and saw how angry he was.

"Just pretend I is a cabbage," said Ginger, curling up into a ball.

"OK," said Maxwell, taking a deep breath. "HOLD ON TO YOUR WHISKERS."

Then he ran forwards and kicked Ginger harder than he had ever kicked anything in his life.

With an ear-splitting *yowl* Ginger hit the window and smashed through it, fragments of glass spraying across the room as he bounced across the carpet. He got up, shook himself, then sprang around the sofa shrieking as if his fur was on fire.

"GET OUT OF HERE, YOU CRAZY CAT!" yelled Dabsley, swinging the axe.

Ginger hissed and knocked over a pair of crystal vases, which fell to the floor and shattered.

Lady Pinkerton screamed.

Then Maxwell leapt through the broken window and skidded across into the shadows of the hall, hoping he wasn't too late.

CHAPTER FOURTEEN
A TERRIBLE DISCOVERY

Maxwell ran through the gloom, breathing the smell of ancient dust that had settled onto carpets and curtains over months and years. He longed to be outside again, tasting the scent of grass and the sweet breath of the wind. But his friends were in danger and there was work to be done.

He ran down the hallway beneath paintings of unsmiling men with bushy beards and ladies in sombre hats. At the end of the corridor was a half-open door, but as he made his way towards it he looked up and saw, to his horror, that the walls were lined with the heads of long-dead animals: moose, elk and red deer stared silently down at him with empty, lifeless eyes.

"MR B!" cried Maxwell, his voice breaking. "MADISON! RESTREPPO! WHERE ARE YOU?"

When he reached the door, he stood on his hind legs and pushed. The door swung open and he stopped, his eyes wide with shock. For there above him, lined up along the wall, were the heads of his friends. Beneath them, neatly presented in small wooden frames, were old-fashioned tea cards with the pictures and names of each breed of dog:

ROTTWEILER, BULL TERRIER,
SPANIEL, DOBERMANN,
DACHSHUND, ALSATIAN,
POODLE, BULLDOG

Maxwell stared at the faces of his friends and realized that he had come too late to save them.

"What have they done to you?" he howled. "What have they done?"

He lay down and covered his eyes with his paws, unable to look at the world any more.

For a few moments, there was only silence.

Then a familiar voice said, "I can't speak for the others, but I expect they put me up here to make the place look gorgeous."

Hardly daring to hope, Maxwell opened his eyes and looked up to see Mr B staring down at him. He shook his head, shut his eyes and then opened them again.

"COO-EE!" said Mr B. **"PEEK-A-BOO!"**

"Mr B!" cried Maxwell. "You're alive!"

"Yeah, worse luck," said Madison, opening one eye. "That dog snores like a sick horse."

"Madison's just peeved because they put his head through a wall," said Mr B. "Messed up his hairdo."

127

"Nothing a dollop of hair gel won't fix," said Dachshund Dan. "Come round when we get back and I"ll sort you out a jar."

"Cheers Dan," said Madison. "It's nice to have *real* friends."

"Friends are all very well," said Mr B. "But what we need is room service."

"I don't understand," said Maxwell. "What's going on?"

The other dogs' eyelids fluttered open and they turned to look at Maxwell.

"It's that Lady Pinkerton," said Restreppo. "She wanted some real dogs to go with her card collection, so Dabsley stuck our heads through a wall to show us off. Humans, eh?"

"It's actually quite comfy," yawned Dave, and Maxwell saw that each dog had a little shelf below its chin with a cushion for its head. "That Ferris

128

boy made these with his tool kit. He seems all right really."

"I'm still gonna bite him," said Madison. "I'm gonna bite everyone."

Mr B looked around at the walls.

"Lady Pinkerton's going to go nuts when she sees what they've done to the place," he said.

There was a shout from the corridor and Maxwell ran to the door to see Dabsley striding up the hallway.

"DABSLEY'S COMING!" he shouted. **"AND HE'S GOT AN AXE!"**

"Head through the wall, man with an axe," said Madison. "What could possibly go wrong?"

"Quickly, Restreppo," said Maxwell. "Tell me what to do!"

"That other door takes you round the back to where the cages are," said Restreppo. "All you have to do is slip the bolts and we're out of here."

Maxwell ran through the door and found himself next to a set of steps which led up to a long wooden platform. Along the top was a series of cages and each one contained the back end of a dog. The nearest one contained the back end of Mr B.

"QUICK!" yelled Mr B from the other side of the wall. "He's coming!"

Maxwell leapt up the steps and tried to pull the bolt with his teeth, but it wouldn't budge.

"Who's first?" shouted Dabsley. "The fancy poodle or the fat bulldog?"

"Who are you calling fat?" cried Mr B. "I'm just big-boned!"

The axe swished and Mr B pulled his head back through the wall, banging it on the edge of the cage. "Maxwell, he's going to chop our heads off!" he yelled. "You have to get us out of here!"

As the other dogs pulled their heads through the wall, Maxwell turned to see a wild-eyed Dabsley staring at him.

"YOU AGAiN!" he spat.

With a sudden surge of strength, Maxwell pulled the bolt back on Mr B's cage and the door sprang open. Dabsley swung the axe onto the platform and the wood splintered, sending both dogs tumbling to the floor.

"Yee-haw!" yelled Dabsley. "Have some of that!"

But as Dabsley lifted the axe once more, Maxwell spun round and sank his teeth into his ankle.

"AAAAARGH!" screamed Dabsley. "Get away from me, you manky little mutt!"

Kicking Maxwell against the wall, he turned and pointed the axe at Mr B. "You! Fat bulldog! Get back in your cage or else!"

"Or else what?" asked Maxwell, calmly taking a step towards him.

"Maxwell, what are you doing?" said Mr B nervously. "He's got an axe."

"I don't care," said Maxwell. "I'm not leaving you this time."

Although his sides were still aching from the kick, he struggled back onto what was left of the platform and made his way towards Restreppo's cage.

"Don't worry, Restreppo," he said. "I'm coming to get you out."

"All right mutt," said Dabsley. "Now you're really asking for it."

But Maxwell just kept walking until he reached Restreppo's cage and took the bolt firmly between his teeth. Then, as Dabsley lifted the axe, he closed his eyes and waited for the end to come.

"STOP!" ordered a voice. "Stop right there!"

Maxwell opened his eyes to see Lady Pinkerton standing in the doorway, pointing a shotgun at Dabsley. Remembering the noise of the guns in Dabsley's cowboy films, he hid behind Restreppo's cage, shaking.

"W-what are you doing?" stammered Dabsley, backing away.

"You can see perfectly well what I'm doing," said Lady Pinkerton. "Now drop the axe."

"What if I don't?"

Lady Pinkerton raised the shotgun higher. "Do you really want to find out?

Dabsley threw the axe to the floor. "I was only doing what you asked me to do," he said.

"I never asked for all *this*," said Lady Pinkerton. "All these dogs trapped in cages. I just wanted..."

"Your trouble is, you don't know what you want," said Dabsley. "Living here all by yourself with your weird collections of bugs, cards and dogs. Now give me the gun, old lady."

Maxwell watched in horror as Dabsley took a step towards her.

"I said, give me the gun."

"I'm warning you, Mr Dabsley. Come any closer and I'll shoot."

"No you won't," said Dabsley. "You haven't got the guts."

But as Dabsley reached out to grab the gun, Maxwell saw Lady Pinkerton's finger tighten on the trigger and knew that, in spite of the horrible things

Dabsley had done, in spite of all his fear, he didn't want Dabsley to die. So with one final effort he pulled the bolt on Restreppo's cage and then raced across the room, leapt into the air and knocked the gun from Lady Pinkerton's hands.

"NO!" she screamed. "You don't understand!"

As the gun clattered to the floor, something in the hallway caught Dabsley's attention.

"Keep your stupid dogs, you daft old bat!" he shouted, snatching up the axe and hurling it through the window.

"FOR GOODNESS' SAKE!" shouted Mr B as the glass shattered. **"WOULD YOU STOP MAKING EVERYTHING SO MESSY!"**

With an angry bark, he threw himself at Dabsley and tore the scarf from his neck.

Dabsley shoved the snarling Mr B aside and jumped through the broken window, disappearing off into the night.

Lady Pinkerton sank to the floor and pushed the gun away. "That gun hasn't worked for years," she said. "It wasn't even loaded."

Maxwell saw a blue light flashing outside and then Restreppo bounded into the hallway shouting, "It's Officer Marshall, it's Officer Marshall!"

"MY BEST BOY!" said Officer Marshall as Restreppo sprang into his arms. "How ever did you get here?"

Maxwell noticed Rosie Morello standing behind Officer Marshall, holding Ginger in her arms. When Ginger saw Maxwell, he gave him a little nod.

"Look who I's findin'," he said.

"This really is an excellent piece of detective work, Miss Morello," said Officer Marshall. "If you hadn't contacted us I don't think we'd ever have found them."

"I'd love to take the credit," said Rosie, "but it was actually the little dog who told me where to find them. It took me a while to work it out, but I got there in the end."

Officer Marshall chuckled. "If only dogs could talk," he said. "The things they could tell us!"

He reached into his top pocket and took out a handful of photographs. "These certainly look like the missing dogs, Miss Morello. And the best missing dog of all is my very own Restreppo. Come here, you little scamp!"

"i KNEW HE LOVED ME REALLY!" yelped

Restreppo, licking Officer Marshall's face. "Officer

Marshall was looking at photographs of the

missing dogs all along!"

Madison's lip trembled and

he suddenly burst into tears.

"Madison," said Mr B

in surprise. "Whatever is

the matter?"

"I'll be fine," said

Madison, pressing his paws

to his eyes. "I just need a moment, that's all."

Dave nodded sympathetically. "Take all the time

you need."

"Now, Lady Pinkerton," said Officer Marshall,

looking at the room full of dogs and the gun on the

floor. "Perhaps you'd like to tell me what's going on?"

To Maxwell's surprise, Lady Pinkerton began to cry. "I never meant to hurt anyone," she said. "It's just that ... having pictures of the dogs was no longer enough."

"What do you mean?" asked Officer Marshall.

"I can't stop *collecting* things," explained Lady Pinkerton, "and recently I decided I needed some real dogs to go with the pictures I collected as a child. I thought that once I had the real dogs it would make me feel better, so I got Mr Dabsley and his boy to help me catch them. But when I saw what he had done to them, especially that beautiful bulldog, I realized I had only made everything worse."

"Did she just call me *beautiful?*" whispered Mr B.

"I think she did," said Dave.

"Trick of the light," said Madison, who had pulled himself together.

"Lady Pinkerton," said Rosie. "I was just wondering – did Mr Dabsley ever bring you a small Pekinese? My dog Paisley is missing and I can't think where to find her."

Lady Pinkerton shook her head. "I'm sorry," she said. "I'm afraid a Pekinese was never on the cards."

"I see," said Rosie, pulling out her handkerchief. She dabbed at her eyes and then stared at Lady Pinkerton. "Tell me something. Why do you love collecting things so much?"

Lady Pinkerton sighed. "Many years ago, I had a sister who collected toy animals. When our parents died, no one would adopt us both so we were sent to live with different families. Before we went our separate ways, I promised her that one day I would find her. But although I tried, I never saw her again.

I broke my promise, you see, and that is a terrible thing."

Lady Pinkerton's eyes filled with tears and she brushed them away with her sleeve.

"I'm sorry," she said. "It's just that collecting things reminds me of her." She sighed. "I remember, when we were young, our mother used to sing the most beautiful song to us before we went to sleep. It was an old Italian lullaby, I think."

Maxwell looked at Rosie and saw how tightly she clasped her handkerchief, turning it over and over in her hands.

"What was your sister's name?" she asked.

"Her name was Rosalind," said Lady Pinkerton. "But everyone called her Rosie."

CHAPTER FIFTEEN

RETURN TO DENBY STREET

"What is I tellin' you?" Ginger whispered as they gathered on the lawn outside. "You is a brave dog, Maxwell Mutt."

Then, as cats often do, he slunk away into the night.

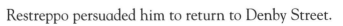

The East Street Dogs begged Maxwell to go back to the alley for a game of football, but Restreppo persuaded him to return to Denby Street.

"Take care of yourselves!" called Madison as

Darlene and her friends disappeared off through the gates. "See you soon, I hope!"

Mr B looked at him.

"What?" snapped Madison.

"Nothing."

Although Dabsley had disappeared, Officer Marshall discovered Ferris potting out geraniums in Lady Pinkerton's shed and got him to fix the broken window. Then he put Maxwell and the Denby Street dogs in the back of his car and drove them all home.

Paisley was still missing, but Rosie Morello was so thrilled to have found her sister after all these years that she was determined to have a party.

"I'm not taking no for an answer, Officer Marshall," she said. "I'm coming to your house to organize things and that is that."

The sun was setting as Rosie, Lady Pinkerton, the dogs and their owners gathered in Restreppo's living room to hear Officer Marshall make a speech.

"You know, we've all lived in this street longer than I can remember," he said, "but in all these years we've hardly spoken to each other. So although it was a bad thing when our dogs went missing, we've all made new friends and that is a very good thing indeed."

"HEAR, HEAR," said Mr and Mrs Durnford of 3 Denby Street, who wore knitted sweaters with poodles on the front.

"HEAR, HEAR," said Mr Bertram of 7 Denby Street, dabbing at his eyes because he had thought Dachshund Dan was lost for ever.

"HEAR, HEAR," said the dogs and they all looked at Maxwell.

"I want to thank you all for coming," continued Officer Marshall, "and to give special thanks to Rosie and her sister, who have organized this wonderful spread." He gestured to a table covered with delicious-looking food. There were plates of sandwiches with the crusts cut off, iced doughnuts sprinkled with hundreds and thousands, mini pork pies with three kinds of pickle and an assortment of chocolate puddings topped with cream.

"And of course, I haven't forgotten our most important guests of all," said Rosie, setting bowlfuls of meaty chunks in front of the hungry dogs.

As the owners laughed and chatted and piled up their plates, Maxwell and his friends huddled together and licked their bowls clean.

Outside, a crescent moon hung low in the sky and the lights were coming on all over the city.

"Where are *your* owners, Mr B?" asked Maxwell when they had finished eating. "Couldn't they come?"

"Oh, I expect they're busy," said Mr B. He stroked the yellow scarf he had stolen from Dabsley. "This is such a soft fabric. I actually think it might be cashmere." He stared through the window at the shadows on the lawn. "Now you come to mention it, I really should be getting back."

"Shush," said Restreppo. "Officer Marshall's talking."

"And now," announced Officer Marshall,

"I have another special treat. Our new friend, Rosie Morello, has agreed to sing for us."

Everyone clapped enthusiastically and Rosie blushed. She mouthed *Thank you* and held up her hands for quiet. Then she began to sing.

"Ninna nanna, ninna oh,
Questo bimbo a chi lo do?
Ninna nanna, ninna oh,
Questo bimbo me lo terrò."

Maxwell remembered hearing the song for the first time and how it had made him think that somewhere, beyond the walls of Dabsley's dark and dingy flat, there was a brighter world.

But now it only reminded him of a broken promise and of what had been lost.

🐾 🐾 🐾

While the others listened, Maxwell crept outside and walked slowly to the end of the garden. As the notes of Rosie's song soothed the sleeping flowers, he sat on the grass and looked up at the sky.

"I'm sorry, Paisley," he whispered.

Somewhere in the darkness, the leaves rustled and a twig snapped.

Something moved in the shadows.

"Hello?" called Maxwell. "Are you looking for someone?"

"I heard the music," replied a small voice. "It reminded me of something."

Maxwell stopped and breathed in the scent of honeysuckle.

"What did it remind you of?" he asked.

For a moment, the night seemed to hold its breath. Then, as light spilled into the garden from an upstairs room, the small figure turned to look at him. "It reminded me of you."

As Maxwell ran faster and faster through the wet grass, Rosie stopped singing and everyone rushed to the windows to see a small dog in the middle of the lawn, its face turned up to the stars while an even smaller dog clung to it as if it would never let go.

"He's found her!" shouted Dachshund Dan. "He's found Paisley!"

"Well, would you look at that," said Restreppo.

He turned to look at Madison. "Are you all right, Madison?"

"I'm fine," said Madison, dabbing at his eyes with the curtain. "It's just been a very emotional day."

CHAPTER SIXTEEN

MR B IS SURPRISED

It was only after Rosie Morello had swept Paisley up in her arms that Maxwell realized Mr B was nowhere to be seen.

Paisley caught Maxwell's eye and mouthed *help me* as Rosie covered her with kisses, but Maxwell could see how happy she was. So while everyone clapped and cheered, he slipped quietly out through the door and into the street. He guessed Mr B just wanted to be back with his owners at the lovely home he had talked about so much.

But why had he left without saying goodbye?

Maxwell ran along the street peering through gates and hedges, hoping to catch a glimpse of Mr B trotting across a lawn or scratching at someone's door.

But there was no sign of him.

After a while, Maxwell came to a house that looked different from the others. The house was in darkness and several of the windows were boarded up. Outside the grass was thick with dandelions and in the middle of the lawn was a wooden sign.

Maxwell was about to turn back when he heard a familiar voice say, "Come on, now. Stay up, stay up."

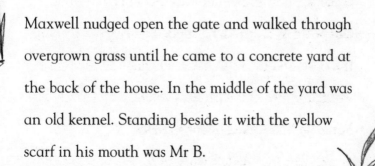

Maxwell nudged open the gate and walked through overgrown grass until he came to a concrete yard at the back of the house. In the middle of the yard was an old kennel. Standing beside it with the yellow scarf in his mouth was Mr B.

Maxwell watched him trying to drape the fabric over the kennel entrance.

"Need any help, Mr B?" he said.

Mr B dropped the scarf and spun around.

"Maxwell! I thought you were still at the party."

"I was," said Maxwell. "I came to see if you were all right." He stared at the concrete yard and the broken down kennel. "Are you all right?"

"I'm just, you know ... fixing things up," said Mr B. "It's amazing how messy a place can get while you're away."

Maxwell looked at the dark house and the empty yard with weeds growing through the concrete.

"I can help if you like."

"No, really, I'm fine. All it needs is a little care and attention."

Mr B stood on his hind legs and hooked the scarf over a rusty nail. Then he sat down and stared at the ground.

"It's no good, Maxwell," he said at last. "I can't pretend any more. I never had any lovely things or a lovely house. That's just how I wanted things to be. But I made them all up." He sighed.

"The truth is, my owners never really wanted me – or each other. So they moved out and left me here with an empty house and a broken kennel."

"And a yellow scarf," said Maxwell. "Don't forget that."

"Look on the bright side, eh?" said Mr B. "You'll go far, Maxwell Mutt."

"Maybe I don't want to go far," said Maxwell.

"Maybe I like it here, what with the yellow scarf and everything." ·

Mr B stared at the scarf. "It *is* very yellow, isn't it?"

"The yellowest," said Maxwell.

He trotted over to the lawn and pulled up some dandelions. "Maybe you could put these in your kennel? Carry on the yellow theme."

"Like sunshine, you mean?" said Mr B. "That would brighten everything up!"

When he had finished decorating the inside of the kennel, Maxwell made a circle of dandelions around the outside.

"*Nice*," said Mr B, nodding approvingly. "Very nice indeed."

"Do you mind *very* much?" asked Maxwell. "About not having a lovely house full of lovely things?"

Mr B stared at the circle of dandelions. "I thought I did," he said. "But with everything that's happened, I've finally realized that all I need is friends."

"That's a shame then," said a voice, and Maxwell turned to see Madison, Paisley and Restreppo walking up the path.

"Why?" asked Mr B. "What are you talking about?"

"Lady Pinkerton has just announced that she's selling her old house," said Paisley. "She says it's too big and expensive to run."

"I can see the dusting must be a nightmare," said Mr B. "But what's it got to do with me?"

"When we drove past earlier, Lady Pinkerton saw the For Sale sign outside this place," said Restreppo. "Now she wants to buy it and live here with her sister. She's going to pay Ferris to help her do it up. And the best bit is, she wants her favourite bulldog to live in it with her."

Mr B frowned. "Does Dave know about this?"

"Oh, for goodness' sake," said Madison. "She's talking about *you*!"

"ME?" said Mr B, pressing a paw to his chest. **"LiTTLE OLD ME?"**

"Hard to believe, I know," said Restreppo, "but she's been looking for you everywhere. And she says she's not going to spare any expense doing this place up and making it look ... what was the word she used, Madison?"

"I think it was *fabulous*," said Madison.

"FABULOUS?" echoed Mr B, dancing around

his kennel. "At last! I'm going to live in a house surrounded by lots of **GORGEOUS, LOVELY, FABULOUS** things!"

"Wait," said Restreppo. "What happened to *All I need is friends?*"

"I may have exaggerated," said Mr B. Then he ran off to choose new colours for the curtains.

As he scampered off, Paisley wandered over to Maxwell and nudged him with her nose. "Thank you," she said.

"For what?"

"If it wasn't for you, I'd never have found my way home. You kept your promise, Maxwell Mutt. And that is the sign of a true friend."

"FRiENDS NEVER GiVE UP," said Maxwell. "Didn't anyone ever teach you that?"

As they sat together side by side, Maxwell thought of all the bad things that had happened. He realized that, somehow, they had brought him here with his friends, looking out across a moonlit garden towards the bright city and the river beyond. He knew there was a part of him that would never be tamed, that one day something would call him back through the gate and out into the world again. But for now he was happy to listen to the sound of paws padding down the street and a familiar voice calling:

"MAXWELL MUTT!
MAXWELL MUTT!
iT'S DARLENE AND THE BOYS.
WE WERE JUST WONDERiNG..."

Maxwell watched the pale moon sail into an inky sky and remembered Ridley's words: *What's lost can be found. And in between the looking there's always fun to be had.*

He looked at the neat rows of cabbages lined up in next-door's vegetable garden, then turned to Paisley.

"This time *you're* on my team," he said. "This time we're definitely going to win."

STEVE VOAKE

is the author of many books for children,

including the **DAISY DAWSON** and **HOOEY HIGGINS**

series. He lives in Somerset with his family,

several woodlice and a small spider called Eric.

JIM FIELD

is a lead-driven, pencil-pushing,

12-volt-DC-enhanced illustrator and animator

of frogs on logs, two-headed dogs, pirate cats

in fog. He's a caffeine-fuelled, bike-pedalling

Led Zeppelin fan living in Paris.

Amen.